Bow-Wow
Bugs a Bug

278

For Sharron

47

www.HarcourtBooks.com

Library of Congress
Cataloging-in-Publication Data
is available upon request.

LC 2006011026
ISBN 978-0-15-205813-5

bus stop

BOW-WOW'S
BUG BEAT

18

For Bud

Designed by Megan Montague Cash

46

Harcourt, Inc.

Orlando • Austin • New York
San Diego • Toronto • London

E G H F D

For Ruby

And for you, too!

Bow-Wow
Bugs a Bug

Mark Newgarden & Megan Montague Cash

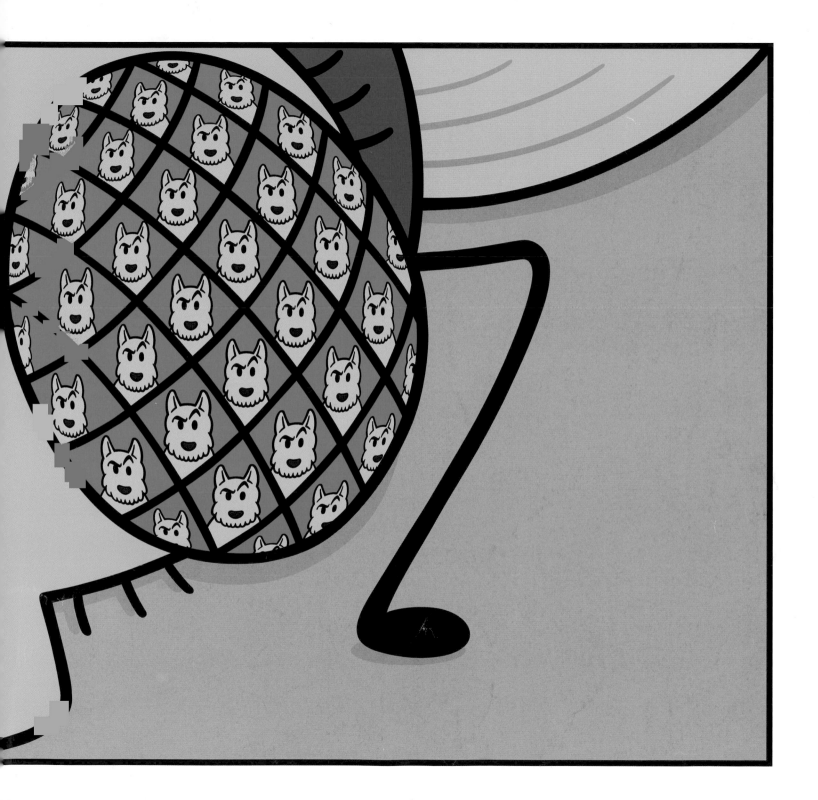

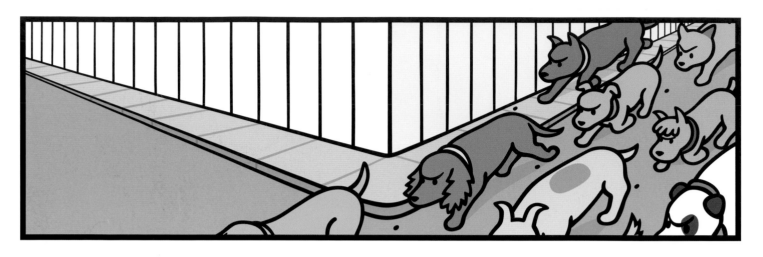

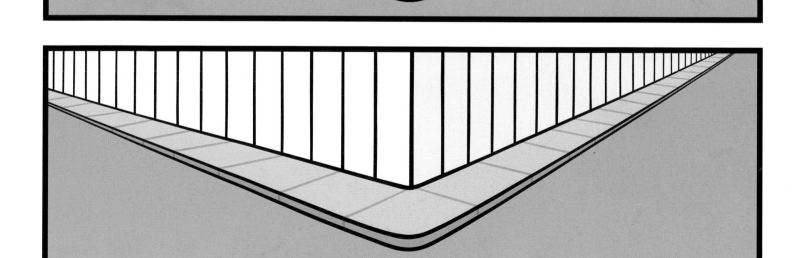

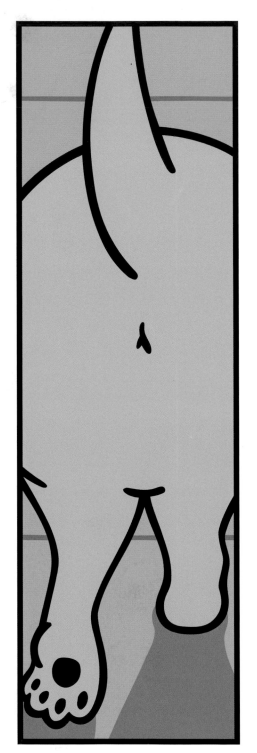

A Bow-Wow Book

www.Bow-WowBooks.com